Mother Fucking
Black Skull of Death

KILLER ENERGY

MATTHEW VAUGHN'S
24 FLUID OUNCES

BIG-AZZ CAN

Mother Fucking Black Skull of Death

By Matthew Vaughn

Mcvaughn138@gmail.com
MorbidbookS.Wordpress.Com
Morbidbooks/facebook.com

MOTHER FUCKING BLACK SKULL OF DEATH

Morbidbooks Is A Grotesque Bizarro Ballet Where The Most Profane Things Occur. An Impious And Perverse Dwelling Of Dark Revulsion. A Cozy Cottage Where Torture Porn And Brutal Bible Tales Are Devised. A Quiet Place To Relax And Spin Tales Of Depravity And Wickedness. A Halfway House For The Disturbed Where Rules No Longer Apply. A Safe Haven For Deviant Serial Killers To Hatch Their Wretched Schemes. Bring Your Pets. The Tasty Ones Are Always Welcome.

ACKNOWLEDGMENTS–

First off I would like to thank William Pauley III again for helping me make my book presentable so I could send it to someone like MorbidbookS. Thanks to Danger Slater for taking the time to read this for me, and for his feedback.

I wrote the first draft of this in March of 2014 while in a Facebook group for writing a Bizarro novella in a month. The encouragement from those involved was invaluable during the early stages of this thing. Thanks to the Grim Reverend Rage and MorbidbookS for putting this book out into the world.

Finally, thanks to my wonderful wife Krystal Vaughn, who supports me and helps me and lets me spend so much of my time with these stories of mine. I love you baby!

PROLOGUE

"Dude, there's a dead body in here," Sam says. He points to a huge vat of neon green liquid. Standing next to him is Rick, the floor manager at Hall Soda Co. "And this drum over here, it's got a big skull and cross bones on it, so you know it can't be good."

"You did the right thing calling me, young man. Now, don't touch any of this without gloves," Rick says. "There's no telling what was in that drum."

"What do you think was going on here?" Sam asks, looking into the vat of liquid.

Rick looks at Sam. He is young, so this is likely his first real job. He dresses like a thug. Rick assumes he probably likes to party, but he likes Sam, and feels he can trust him.

"Son, I think this man was poisoning this batch of drink," Rick put his hand on Sam's shoulder. "I need your help."

Sam could tell Rick was serious, and he liked Rick. He had been good to him in the short amount of time he worked there.

"What do you need, boss? I'll help you out."

"We need to take care of this situation, but we need to do it secretly," Rick says. He points at the man inside the tank. "We need to get this body out of here and drain and clean this tank."

Rick looks Sam in the eyes.

"We can't let anyone know about this," Rick says. "This could ruin Hall Soda Co. If you'll help me cover this up, I'll make it worth your while."

"Sure thing, boss. We can do this," Sam says excitedly.

"Good boy. Now, what's in this vat here?" Rick says. He walks over to a clipboard hanging nearby.

"This is *Mother Fucking Black Skull of Death*," Sam says, before Rick could even read it. "Man, I love that name!"

"It says the last shipment went out to Shelbyville, Kentucky," Rick says, as he flips through the papers on the clipboard. "Well, I'm sure that truck went out before all this happened. I'd say you found this just in time."

Rick drops the clipboard. Sam smiles proudly as Rick slaps his upper back.

"Alright, son, let's get started. We have about four hours before the next crew clocks in."

STEVIE

Mother Fucking Black Skull of Death, that's what the 22 oz. can Vince's holding up to my face says.

"This is what real men drink, you fuckin' pussy," Vince says. He slaps the bottle of Deer Park spring water out of my hand and I watch as liquid splashes from the bottle onto the pavement. "Not that flavored water crap. This is why you're a nerd, Stevie. You're so lame."

The two goons that flank either side of Vince laugh it up. *Yeah, Vince is just so funny, so cool.* Really, he's just a dick.

"That stuff isn't any good for you, Vince," I say. I reach down and pick up my now empty bottle. I need to make sure it ends up in a recycling bin. "Your body needs water, not the toxins and junk that stuff has in it."

Vince takes a big chug from the can, emptying it. He crushes it with one hand and launches it at me. It hits me on the forehead and bounces off. Vince and his goons laugh.

"God, you're such a dweeb," Jeff, one of the goons, says. All three are practically falling over laughing when the door to Mr. Potato-Head's Ball Cards and Comics opens. The only person in town who was more of a loser than me walked out right at that very moment. Hairy Harold Harrison. *Who would name their poor kid Harold Harrison? And what are the chances that the poor kid would end up actually being ridiculously hairy?*

"Hey, Hairy!" Vince says when he sees the kid. "I need another Black Skull of Fucking Death! Give me some money, fucker!"

Hairy Harold pulls the comic books he's holding in his hands up to his chest, and looks cautiously at us. Vince and his goons walk away from me and towards poor Harold.

"I don't have any money on me," Harold says. I feel bad for the dork, but I'm happy he's taking the attention away from me.

"Bullshit," Vince says. He moves closer to Harold and grabs the comics away from him. "What do we have here?"

Harold reaches out to grab the comics, but Vince turns away while one of the goons, Craig, pushes Harold to the ground.

"Let's see, Wolverine and The X-Men, Wolverine and The Avengers, Wolverine and Other Heroes," Vince reads off. "Why the fuck is Wolverine in all these comics? Jeez, comics are getting fucking stupid. Wolverine and the Wolverine Team? How lame is that?"

Vince tosses the comics on the ground. Harold tries to get up but Craig puts his foot on his chest. Vince unbuckles his belt. My instinct tells me to run away now while I have the chance, but I can't help wanting to see what this nutcase is going to do next.

"I'm giving you one last chance to give me some money, loser, or I'm gonna take a shit on your comic books," Vince says. "Come on, geek. I gotta get me some fuckin' Black Skull!"

"Aw no, come on!" Harold pleads. He's tearing up. "Please, I don't have any money!"

"Okay, be like that," Vince drops his pants. He has no shame, letting his penis and testicles hang out for the world to see. He squats over the comic books and grunts.

Jeff and Craig laugh at this like it is comedic genius. I was stunned. I can't believe Vince is actually going to do it. I don't know why I'm surprised, as he does a lot of crazy stuff. He does whatever he wants because his dad runs the town. Vince gets away with everything. That's why when Mrs. Crabtree comes walking by with her miniature poodle, and sees Vince squatted with a runny turd exiting his rear, she just pulls the little dog across the street. And speaking of Vince's poop, it can't be healthy to have feces that look like that. The color and consistency, like neon green toxic oatmeal, has to be coming from that energy drink he loves so much. I watch as the brightly colored, runny mess exits his butthole and lands with a wet splat on the newest issue of "Wolverine Presents: Tales of Wolverine."

"Ew dude, that's just sick!" Jeff says. He's still laughing though. Vince picks up one of the only comics to not have any poop on it, "Galactic Wolverine and Friends," and runs it between his butt cheeks to clean off any remaining diarrhea. He bends over to collect the feces covered comics. His pants are still around his ankles, so we get a full view of his hairy butt, brown eye and all, which, by the way, still has plenty of crap on it that needs to be wiped off.

"Here ya go, buddy. Here's your comics back," Vince says to Hairy Harold. He laughs as he tosses the books, poop side down, and they land on Harold's face. I can't help but gag. I almost can't choke it back. That's just gross.

"Oh my god, dude! That was the greatest thing I've ever seen!" Jeff says.

"Dude! Dude! He's gonna puke!"Craig says. He is backing away from Harold, who has rolled over onto his hands and knees. He is dry heaving, and it sounds awful.

"Hey guys, check it out!" Vince says. He's holding a few bucks in his hand. "Looks like I had some money in my pocket after all!"

The three of them run up and high five each other. They head off towards the Marathon gas station. I look down at Hairy Harold. He's done puking, but he's laying there crying. I feel bad for him. A part of me thinks maybe I should do something. I don't know what to do, so I just leave. *What could I really do for the kid anyway?* You know what I mean. Shit, I wasn't gonna touch that weird colored poop, or buy him new comics. Besides, I needed to get over to the community college. I have a paper due, but I also have some experiments to get out of the way first. Professor Johnson is only going to allow me access to the chemistry lab for a few more hours.

<u>*VINCE*</u>

This bitch is really going to town on my dick. She loves this shit. But she's starting to gag, so I grab her head. I don't want her to back off before I'm done. She is definitely trying to pull away, so I hold on and just start fucking her face. She's smacking my legs and still gagging. I hear Jeff and Craig laughing, so I give them a big smile. Yeah, this shit is awesome.

"Dude, she's gonna puke!" Jeff says. I look down and notice her dry heaving. The sounds coming from this bitch are crazy, but I'm not done yet, so I don't let go. Then it happens, she starts spraying shit out of her nose! Fucking puke is coming out around my dick! She's choking and gagging, and vomit is running down her face!

"That's the most disgusting thing I've ever seen!" Craig says. He's laughing his ass off.

I've got a hold of this bitch's head with a death grip, and I'm using the puke as a lube. I'm slamming it home until finally I bust a nut in her mouth. She still has a mouthful of her vomit, so there's not much room for my spunk in there. A mixture of the two rolls out the sides of her mouth around my cock. I pull out and shove her head away. She falls to the floor, hacking, trying to get all the puke out of her mouth.

"I thought you were a pro?" I ask her. "Clean yourself up. You've still got two more dicks to suck."

She looks up at me and her eyes are red from crying. She knows better than to say anything though, especially if she wants to get paid. I know she does, because surely she's fiending for some meth, or H, or whatever. I watch her go into the bathroom. Her naked ass looks pretty tight. I sit down in the chair. I'm naked and have her puke on me, but I don't give a fuck. I just want another Mother Fucking Black Skull of Death. That shit is good. I look up at Craig as he is sitting on the arm of the chair. He's naked too and his big cock is rock-hard.

"You ready for some of that?" I say and smack his rod. He laughs and hands me a Black Skull. "Fuck yeah! I might just suck your dick!" I grab his cock and give it a couple quick strokes and we laugh.

"Nah, Jeff gets her next," he says. They usually play this game where they watch me fucking a chick and whoever gets hard first is the loser and has to go last. I always go first, know that shit!

"This bitch needs to hurry, yo!" Jeff says. He's standing near her puke, chugging a Black Skull of Death and stroking his rock-hard dick.

"You better not blow your load before she comes out!" I say. We laugh and she stumbles out of the bathroom. I wonder if she can fit both our dicks in her mouth at the same time. She gets down in front of him and starts working his shlong.

We wear this bitch out for awhile. It turns out she *can* get both mine and Jeff's dick in her mouth. We let her get stoned, and then went on to find out how much shit we can stuff inside her pussy and asshole. One of my favorite things to do is stick a finger in both Craig and Jeff's assholes and play *whoever gets hard first loses*. It's Craig again. I'm starting to wonder if the dude's gay, so I have him bend over and I shoot a load in his ass, and then made this high-as-fuck bitch suck that shit out! It was awesome!

Now she's curled up on the bathroom floor, naked and passed out from meth or whatever. I'm standing over her, pissing all over her naked body, when Craig almost knocks me down.

"I need to shit, out of the way!" he says. He drops his drawers and squeezes one out on her chest. I start laughing and my piss sprays all over the place. I accidentally get some on him. "Hey, watch it, fucker!"

MOTHER FUCKING BLACK SKULL OF DEATH

Craig puts his hand underneath his ass and shits in it, and then he launches it at me. I duck, but some of the shit hits my shoulder and we laugh.

We leave that bitch in the hotel, covered in piss, shit, and all the money we owed her. We're not total dicks — we pay. However, she just might have to remove some of the bills from up inside her.

We head down to the local Huck's, after having cleaned Marathon out of all its Black Skull. Stupid fuckin' Ahmed, who runs that store, he needs to order more of that shit next time.

We're not even ten steps inside Huck's and I'm already raging. I can see the cooler where they keep the Mother Fucking Black Skull of Death and it's empty.

"Where the fuck is my drink?" I yell. I want to rip my clothes off and start destroying the store. Jeff runs up to the cooler and starts throwing doors open.

"Aww, no, where is it?" he says. Craig is at the counter, banging on the hard surface.

"Carl! Suzan! Who's working today?" he yells. "We need some fuckin' Death Skull!"

Josh comes out from the back. He's a loser stoner dude. I don't have a problem with him. I've fucked his sister a couple times and let him watch and jerk off.

"Hey Vince, what's happening?" he asks. He looks baked.

"Dude, Black Skull of Death, where is it?" I ask.

"Man, they shorted us in the last shipment, so we sold out. It happened to everybody in town," he says. He fidgets with some of the crap on the counter. I feel as if he's not taking this as seriously as he should be. I grab him by the shirt and push his face against the counter.

"Are you fuckin' with me?" I say into his ear.

"Nah, Vince, I wouldn't fuck with you, man," he says. He holds his hands up as if he's surrendering, like it matters to me if he's had enough.

"Dude!" Jeff yells from behind me. "Check it out, man!"

I turn to see what Jeff is going on about. He's looking out one of the big windows in the front of the store. I follow his gaze and see it, the most beautiful sight. I'm telling ya, you wouldn't believe it.

Pulling into the parking lot is a massive semi, with a huge trailer painted with gory pictures of impaled bodies and a pile of severed heads. There's a huge silver skull near the back that has the words 'Mother' and 'Fucker' where its eye sockets should be, and 'Black Skull of Death' for a mouth. The truck pulls around, away from the front of the store. I can see the doors on the back of the trailer as the driver backs the rig towards us. It's a painting of a naked woman with huge tits. She's covered in blood and sitting on a massive pile of skulls, holding a can of Mother Fucking Black Skull of Death between her legs. I'm instantly hard as a rock.

"Fuck yeah, guys. Let's go!" Craig says as he runs out the door. I let go of Josh. I don't even look at him. I keep my eyes on the truck. The door to the cab opens and a long-legged babe with curly, brown hair climbs out. I don't even care about her; we're just like some puppy dogs begging for that Black Skull treat.

She smiles as she walks past us. Oh yeah, she wants this dick. I'll give it to her too, but only after I get some Black Skull shit. We watch that tight ass as she reaches up and unlatches the trailer doors.

STEVIE

I open my eyes and I'm on the floor. I don't know where I am. My head hurts and when I try to sit up I get dizzy. I power through it and look around. I'm in the lab at school. Oh yeah, I was working on an experiment. It apparently didn't go well. I'm not sure what went wrong, I just remember my chemical compound exploded. I must have fallen off my stool, which would explain why my head hurts. I must have blacked out after that.

I get up from the floor and inspect my body. The chemical compound had to have drenched me when it exploded, but nothing on me is wet. How long was I out for? The clock on the wall says eight thirty-three, so I've been here for three hours. I know I've been working for at least an hour and a half, so that means I couldn't have been out for more than an hour and a half. Was that enough time for my compound to completely dry up?

I decide to call it a night on experiments. I feel kind of weird. I can't fully explain it to you, but I just feel … *off*, you know? Maybe I have a concussion. I clean up the equipment and lock up the lab for Mr. Johnson. I figure I'll just go home and try to figure what went wrong tomorrow.

Outside, the sun is setting, and the slivers of brightness hurt my eyes. Lucky for me, home isn't too far away. I stumble through the fairly empty streets. I do hear some commotion, a couple of people laughing and having a good time. I can't tell where it's coming from, but it doesn't matter. I just want to go home, lie down, and get some sleep.

I turn a corner and spot the laughing people. It's Vince, Jeff, and Craig. I'm so surprised by their presence that I almost fall down.

"Hey, look who the fuck it is!" Vince says. He has a cardboard box on his left shoulder and an energy drink in his hand.

"Little nerdy ass Stevie," Jeff said. I take a step back, thinking I could try to run away, but Craig is behind me. When did he get behind me?

"Where do you think you're going, queer?" Craig asks. He shoves me towards the other two and I lose my footing and fall down. Jeff is on me in an instant. He sits on my stomach, pinning my arms underneath his legs, and knocks the air out of me. The next thing I know, Vince's bare butt is in my face and I'm praying that he doesn't poop on me. His butt stinks like he doesn't wipe very well. He doesn't poop, thankfully. Instead, he seems content just rubbing his balls against my mouth and chin. The three of them are laughing it up. I'd like to breathe, but I don't want to smell Vince's stinky butt anymore. Finally, he stands up and I try to catch my breath.

"I got a special surprise for you, nerd boy," Vince says. I hear the sound of a can being opened, I'm afraid I know where this is going. "I hope you're thirsty."

"Man, don't give him all of it. We don't want to run out again," Jeff says.

"Shut up," Vince says. "I bought it, so fuck you."

Craig chuckles. Jeff puts his head down and pouts. Vince comes back into view, and is now standing over top of me.

"Open wide, fucker, I know you hate this shit," he says. I start thrashing my head around, trying to keep that nasty stuff from getting in my mouth. "Get over here and hold him still!"

Craig comes over and kneels down next to my head. He grabs my hair and holds me in place, pulling my head back and forcing my mouth open.

When it hits, it's awful. The liquid filled my mouth and I was forced to swallow it. It tasted like medicine. It was trying to disguise its awful taste with some off-brand citrus flavor. I gagged and spit some of it out. Vince punched me in the stomach. More drink went down my throat and into my lungs. I thought I might drown. Once the can was empty, Vince crushed it and threw it at my face. They got off of me and I rolled over on my side, coughing and gagging.

"You better not puke that shit up," Vince says. "I'll make you lick your puke back up. You're not wasting my Black Fuckin' Skull of Death."

His goons were laughing. They all reached into the cardboard box and pulled a can out. Just hearing the sounds of the aluminum tops being opened made my stomach turn.

"Is it just me, or do the ones we bought from Huck's taste a little different?" Craig asked. Jeff nodded his head.

"Quit being a little bitch," Vince said. "This shit tastes fine." However, as he took another drink, the look on his face told a different story.

"Yeah, you're just being a bitch," Jeff said, even though he too was looking at his can with a weird look on his face.

"Fuck you, dude!" Craig says to him. He takes a step towards Jeff. Vince steps in front of him.

"Come on, we don't have time for you two to jerk each other off," he says. "That delivery chick told us she was having people over at her house at ten. I'm ready to go fuck some bitches!"

"Hell yeah!" Jeff says. They high five each other and yelled and grabbed dicks, each other's, not their own, as they walked away.

I lay on the ground until I was sure they were gone. I'm dying to get something to wash this awful taste out of my mouth. I don't know how they drink this stuff.

JANET

I hate watching Stevie get picked on by Vince and his gang of bullies. I don't know what it is about putting your ass and dick on people that they think is so funny. I feel bad for Stevie, and for Harold Harrison. I heard what Vince did to him. Disgusting.

I see Stevie on the ground from the window of my bedroom. I want to go out and help him, comfort him, but I'm afraid to. He's so cute, and smart. He probably doesn't even know I exist. When we were in high school together, I had a couple classes with him and he never acknowledged my existence. I'm just a little Goth nobody.

I sit at the window and watch Stevie from afar, like I always have. He gets up slowly, he's a little unsteady, and starts walking away. He's probably going home, judging by the direction he's headed.

"You're always moping around, thinking about that boy who won't even give you the time of day," Stacy says. I turn and look at her sitting on my bed. Stacy is a little stuffed doll that has been my best friend since I was a little girl. "You have so many other boys that do have the time for you."

"They only have time for me because they want to sleep with me," I tell her.

"So, it's not your fault you're so good at sucking dick, or that you let just about anybody put their thing in your butt," she says. "Oh wait, yes it is."

Stacy is such a bitch. I don't know if it's because she's a stuffed doll and doesn't have any feelings or what.

"Thanks for that, you little bitch," I say to her. I have to resist the urge to pick her up and launch her at the wall.

"You know very well that she is trying to change, to get away from her past," Mr. Snugs says. He's a stuffed bear, barely peeking out from the covers. He's scared of everything. Sometimes I wonder if Stacy abuses him when I'm not around.

"I don't see why," Stacy says. "When you're good at something, you should embrace it."

"I don't want to be a whore!" I shout.

"Keep it down in there, Janet!" My mom is yelling from the other room.

"Sorry Mom!"

"You can't change who you are," Stacy says. "Maybe if you hadn't sucked that first dick in sixth grade, your life would be different."

"But Mr. Frederickson was so kind to me. He always helped me out in the locker room after gym," I say. Stacy doesn't understand how good it feels when people treat you nice.

"Don't listen to her, Janet. You can change," Mr. Snugs says. Stacy shoots him a dirty look.

"Thank you Mr. Snugs," I say. I pick up the pack of cigarettes and my cell phone. "I'm gonna go out for a little bit. I need to take a walk and clear my head."

As I close the door behind me, I hear Stacy shouting.

"Try not to fall onto any cocks while you're out!"

That little bitch.

VINCE

This chick is taking my dick like a champ. Her big ol' titties are bouncing all over the place while I'm ramming it in her. I'm giving her pussy a beating and she loves it. I stop in mid-thrust as a weird spasm courses through my body. She gives me a mean look.

"You better not be finished already," she says.

"What?! Fuck no. I just feel a little strange," I tell her and start pounding again. "I got more for you, you dirty bitch."

"Oh yeah, fuckin' give it to me, you piece of shit!" she yells back.

This bitch is on fire, she is fuckin me like a pro! I break out into a sweat, not from this work out, though. I'm burning up, I literally feel on fire. I want to bust my nut all up inside her and a pain shoots throughout my body. I dig my fingers into her thighs and arch my back. A low growl comes out of my mouth.

"Don't you fuckin' stop. I will fuckin' stab you, you fuck," she says. I don't stop, but my muscles are twitching and spasming, and in intense pain. I look down and see my hands are swelling, it's like I've been stung by a swarm of bees. Then, they get all weird and ragged looking, like there are rocks underneath my skin.

The bitch stops moving and her eyes go wide. She mouths *what the fuck* right before she starts screaming. I keep fucking her. I just can't stop, it's like my body won't let me! There's screaming and crying coming from somewhere else in the house. I see something poking this bitch's lower stomach from the inside. I think it's my dick! My neck and shoulders are in agony, the pain is intense! It feels as if my bones are rearranging themselves. I'm gripping her legs tight, pulling them to each side. I see the skin above her slit start to rip. Her head is flopping around and her eyes are barely open. I think I'm fucking her to death! I can't stop myself from pounding her, and as I do so, her legs are pulling even farther apart. The skin is tearing up her belly and blood is pouring out. She's not moving anymore, I'm pretty sure she just died. Who could live after being ripped open like this? Again, I can hear screaming and growling coming from somewhere outside the bedroom door.

I can feel I'm about to finish. The bitch's body is ripped up to her ribcage and all her fuckin' inside shit is spilling out everywhere! I let out a massive roar as I bust my nut into her dead body.

I pull my gore covered dick out and it's massive! I had a nice big cock before, but this thing is a monster and it's covered in rock-looking wart things. My dick is now as big and long as an arm. It's at least a couple feet long! My arms are freakin' massive too. Bigger than any muscle-bound wrestler I've ever seen! I turn away from where this dead bitch lay on the bed. There's a huge dresser by the door and it has a huge mirror on it. I look at my reflection and holy shit! It's not even me! Or rather, it's the new me. I don't fucking know. I'm a freakin' crazy-ass monster, gray and huge. The rocky, wart shit is covering my entire body. I look like a cross between the Incredible Hulk and The Thing, if they were chopped up and glued back together, like a frankenhulk! I need another fuckin' Black Skull of Death! I tear the door off as I exit the room. I'm fucking crazy strong now.

In the living room, there was a party going on, but now there are only ripped up bodies, blood, and shit everywhere, and five crazy-looking giant fucks, just like me. I can kinda tell who Craig and Jeff is, but who are these three other crazy-looking fucks?

"What the fuck is going on?" I ask. My voice sounds like demon who gargled acid.

"I don't know, shit just started getting crazy out of nowhere," one of the crazy-looking fucks says. I'm pretty sure it is Jeff.

"I need a black fuckin' skull! Where are they?" I ask.

"I think we drank them all," Craig says.

"Who the fuck is *we*?" I ask.

"All of us standing here," Jeff says. "I gave those two bitches some and also that dude over there." He points to the three monstrous fuckers that I don't recognize. So now there's me, my boys Jeff and Craig, and a dude and two chicks I don't know. Holy shit; there are six of us fucking monsters!

"What the fuck does it matter to you anyway?" the dude says. "You got a fuckin' problem?"

I guess this badass monster shit went to this motherfucker's head. He doesn't realize I'm the baddest motherfucking monster around.

I run up to him, grab his face, and slam him onto the ground. I kick him in the ribs over and over until he rolls over onto his back. As soon as I see his face, I start pounding away on his ugly mug. He's losing teeth left and right. I'm fucking his face up so bad that he looks even more hideous now.

Jeff and Craig are on this dude too. I didn't even realize at first. These two motherfuckers have my back at all times. I don't care if Jeff might be gay.

"The only fucking problem I have is when somebody thinks they are badder than me," I tell the dude. All his big talk is gone now. "I run this shit, do you hear me? Don't you fuckin' forget it!"

I grab this dude's fucked up face and shove my huge monster dick in his mouth. He starts to squirm, trying to fight me off, but Jeff and Craig hold him down. I hear the two monster bitches behind me; groaning and egging me on while I'm face-fucking this dude. I knocked so many of his teeth out that I don't have to worry about him trying to bite my shit. I pound away at his mouth until I feel like I'm gonna cum. I pull my rock-hard, wart-covered cock out of his mouth and shoot my shit all over his face. Everybody is laughing. It's a fucking riot.

"Alright motherfuckers," I say as I stand up from my fuck toy. "Let's go get some Mother Fucking Black Skull of Death!"

STEVIE

I toss and turn in my bed. I want to sleep, I know I need to sleep, but it just isn't happening. I'm drenched in sweat, and my muscles and bones are in terrible pain. My stomach aches, but not from sickness, it craves something. I can't seem to rid the taste of that energy drink from my mouth. When I think about it, my stomach rumbles. Is that what it wants, that nasty energy drink?

I roll over to the edge of the bed and put my hand on the table where I keep a small lamp and my alarm clock. My hand is huge! I am so shocked to see it that I fall off the bed. I try using the table to catch myself and it splinters apart with ease. I land with a loud thud that shakes my bed. I lay there for a second expecting to hear my mom screaming at me through the wall. She doesn't, so she must be into a deep alcohol-induced coma.

I stand on wobbly legs, my head still pounding, and my muscles still burning. I grab the door knob with my enormous mitt and crush it in my grip. Barely pulling on the door knob causes it and a good chunk of the door to splinter off. With the latch now missing, the door lazily opens. I toss the piece of door onto the bed and walk to the bathroom to check myself out in the mirror.

I try to be quiet and sneak through the house, but every step I take sounds like I'm trying to stomp through the floor. I push open the bathroom door and click on the light. I am not prepared for what I see. I look like a body builder. I'm freakin' huge! My skin has a strong reddish tint to it and my eyes have become yellow, devoid of irises. To me I look like a muscle-bound demon.

The hunger consumes me and I lean over on the sink. The porcelain breaks off the wall. I'm lucky no pipes break. I have to get some of that Black Skull. As awful as it is, this intense craving is worse.

I exit the bathroom and almost trample my mother.

"Oh crap, I'm sorry," I say to her. She looks frightened at first, and then she looks me up and down.

"I don't know how you got in here," my mom said in her trademark drunken slur. "But now that you're here, you want to fuck?"

"Mom! What's wrong with you? It's me, Stevie," I say to her. She reaches out and grabs my penis, and that's when it hits me — I'm naked. I smack her hand away. She smiles at me and I'm sick seeing my thing get hard.

"My boy's name is Stevie," she says. She rubs on herself in sexual ways. It's really gross. "We need to be quiet so we don't wake him."

My mom is squeezing on her boobs and my penis is as hard as a rock. I push past her. I want to throw up.

"Wait, come back! I want that hard dick in me!" Mom yells after me. "You got me all wet with that big cock of yours!"

That is the last thing I hear as I smash through the front door and run out into the night.

It's cool out, and being naked feels great. The sweat that was covering my body is drying up and is starting to make me a little chilly. My erection finally went down. I'm happy about that because running with a hard on swinging is kind of weird.

I try to stay out of sight. Being a massive red-skinned dude is one thing, but to be naked on top of that is just asking for trouble. I stay close to buildings and try to hide in the shadows. I peer around corners to make sure the coast is clear before I go very far. The Marathon is just a few more blocks, if I can maintain not being seen, I might be alright.

I guess I get distracted inside my thoughts, because as I turn a corner I almost squash a girl. I stop just in time, so she is fine. I recognize her. We went to school together and had some of the same classes. She is taken aback by my appearance. Then I see her eyes move down to my crotch. Her eyes get big and I cover myself in embarrassment.

"I'm sorry, excuse me," I say. The voice that comes out of my mouth surprises me every time I speak. I kinda sound like Pete from those Mickey Mouse cartoons.

"No, that's okay," she says. She squints her eyes and looks at my face. "Stevie, is that you?"

I didn't think I resembled my old self that much. I also didn't know she knew my name. No girls ever seemed to know my name.

"Yeah, it's me," I shifted uncomfortably in my nakedness. "How do you know who I am?"

It almost seemed like she was blushing. The bad lighting and my new eyes were making it difficult to tell.

"I've known who you were for a long time," she says. She fumbles in her pockets and produces a cigarette pack and a lighter. "We had some classes together in high school. I used to sit behind you."

"I know who you are," I tell her. Of course I know who she is, but girls have never paid much attention to me.

"Then how come you never said anything to me in school?"

"I don't usually talk to girls. I'm kinda shy. I especially have a problem with pretty girls, like you." Now I'm probably blushing, I can't believe I said that. "Plus, you were popular. Guys were always talking to you."

"That doesn't mean I was popular. Guys only wanted to get one thing from me," she says. She looks sad. I want to console her, but I don't know how to deal with these kinds of situations. Plus, I'm naked and covering my junk, what could I really do? "None of those guys were my friends. I never really had any friends, just Stacy and Mr. Snugs."

"I know how you feel. I never had any real friends either," I tell her. I'm starting to feel more comfortable around her. She seems to like me. "I always buried myself in books and school work. Wait, who's Mr. Snugs? Sounds like a stuffed animal or something."

"Well, maybe I can introduce you to him one day," she says. She drops her cigarette to the ground and stamps it out with her combat boot. I watch her as she raises her head and stares at me. I look down. Crap. I forgot to keep my penis covered. This is ridiculous.

MOTHER FUCKING BLACK SKULL OF DEATH

"We need to get you some clothes," she said. She reaches up and grabs one of my hands, which makes it difficult to keep my junk covered with only one hand, but whatever.

I allow her to pull me along, but I try to stay alert. I don't want to run into someone and freak them out. Then, out of nowhere, a pain attacks my stomach and I let go of her hand to double over.

"Are you okay?" she asks. There is genuine concern in her voice. I like that.

"I was going to get an energy drink. My body is craving it," I tell her once I can catch my breath.

"Energy drink? That's oddly specific."

"Yeah, it's that Black Skull of Death drink. I think that is what changed me into this."

"Really? How is that?" she asks, clearly skeptical. Another round of pain hits me and I let out a yell.

"I don't know. All I know is that's what I'm craving," I say to her. "My body wants it. I think it will feed my transformation."

"Okay, that's cool," she says. She takes my hand again. I have my other on my stomach, so there goes modesty. "Come on, that Marathon is just around the corner."

We walk towards the Marathon, moving a little quicker than before. I don't care so much about hiding in the shadows right now. I need to get fed. It's the only thing important to me at the moment.

Janet says she will go in and buy me some, so I sit behind the building, in the dark. It's easy to forget that I'm a big, strong thing now. Sitting alone in the dark, my paranoia hits hard. I hear every little sound. Is that a Rat? Is somebody behind that dumpster? My first thought would be Vince, ready to jump out and beat me up or poop on me, as I've seen him do to others. There were also rumors around school that he did some other things to kids, awful things. Supposedly there was this dude, real nerdy, like me, and Vince and his friends caught him alone in the woods behind the school. They stripped him naked, beat him senseless, and shoved different objects up his ass and into his pee hole.

I also heard he had a tendency to have sex with guys against their will, but he acts like he hates gay people. I never knew the kid they tortured in the woods. I don't even know for sure he existed.

I hear a noise. I start to panic. There really isn't any place to hide.

"Okay, here you go," she says and I scream. It's just Janet. "Whoa, calm down, Stevie!"

"Sorry, being out here alone in the dark was freakin' me out," I tell her. She hands me a 24 oz can of Black Skull of Death. I can't open it fast enough.

"You know you are bigger and scarier than anything out here, right?" she says to me. I don't answer, I'm too busy chugging this drink. It is really hitting the spot. It tastes awful, but it's exactly what my body was craving.

JANET

I can't believe my luck, running into Stevie like this, in a time he needs my help. It's like a dream come true. Sure, he doesn't look the same, but really he's pretty wicked looking. I can't help glancing at that shlong he's packing. I try to stop myself, I really am trying to change my ways. But when it's just hanging out there like that, I can't help it.

"I don't know why, but this is making me feel better and stronger," Stevie says between drinks.

"I've never really liked those things," I say, trying to fill the awkward silence, but I guess I'm just not that interesting. "What do you think is up with them anyway?"

"Honestly, I don't know," he says. "There's this guy, Vince. I don't know if you know him or not. He's a real dick. He hangs out with these other two jerks, Jeff and Craig."

"Uh, yeah, I know who you're talking about," I say. What I won't say is anything about that night with Vince and his friends. What I did or what they made me do. Stevie doesn't need to know about all that.

"Well, they forced me to drink this stuff and I went home to sleep, but then this happened to me," he says. "Something in it must have had some weird reaction to my body."

He sits up, looking like he suddenly realizes something, but before he can say anything we turn towards some very loud voices. It sounds like demons are walking the earth. We peak around the corner. There are five monstrous-looking things coming this way. They look insane, like huge deformed steroid abusers from some dark fantasy realm.

"What in the world?" Stevie says. I don't say anything. I just watch these things. Three of them have very large penises, but they are covered with bumps. The other two are clearly female. Their large breasts give that away.

"I need me some fuckin' black skull!" the lead monster says. I don't know how I know this, but I'm sure it's Vince.

"Vince," Stevie says beside me. We watch as they smash their way into the Marathon, screaming and yelling. "How many people were in the store when you went in?"

"I only saw two," I say. "The guy behind the counter and another standing there talking to him"

"Let's see if we can peek through a window and see what they are doing," Stevie says.

"Okay, but let's be extra careful," I say. I inch towards the nearest window. "Those guys were crazy before, there's no telling what they are like now."

We reach the closest window and peer inside. I can only see the one guy in there, not the cashier. He's at the counter, frozen stiff. He looks like he might have pissed his pants. The monsters are chugging drinks like they are going out of style.

One of the female creatures is eyeballing the poor guy standing in there.

"I want to eat this motherfucker," she says as she walks towards him.

"I'm so fucking hard right now!" Vince says. He starts walking up behind the female and I can see he's stroking his large cock.

She picks the guy up by his neck, and then Vince rams her from behind. She swings around and the guy's arms are flailing like crazy. She grabs Vince by the face and pulls his head into her breasts. She's growling and the guy is turning red in the face.

Vince pulls his head up and forces the female to turn around. She does, and Vince wastes no time in shoving his dick into her. I feel so bad for the poor guy. While Vince is slamming it to that female, that guy is getting thrown around and slammed into the counter. He looks like he can't breathe.

The female is growling and gnashing her teeth, and then suddenly she grabs the guy's head and rips it off at the neck. I contain a scream. She turns the headless body upside-down and lets the blood pour all over her. Vince is howling and growling. This whole deal is so twisted.

Stevie isn't saying a word. He must be just as mortified as I am. I can't even turn my head away to look at him. Then a monster pops up in front of us and points at Stevie. We don't even have a chance to react. The monster punches through the glass. I scream as I'm showered with shards.

I open my eyes and see Stevie being dragged through the window. I scream and massive, scaly hands wrap around me and pull me inside too!

"Look what the fuck I just found!" the monster says.

Stevie smacks the monster's hands off him. He is equally as big as Vince and his friends, but he doesn't look as crazy and scary as they do.

"Watch yourself, big man," the monster says. He holds me up between him and Stevie. "I've got your girlfriend. I'll squish her fucking head if you move!"

He has me around the head. I can't even warn Stevie about the monster coming up behind him. It's another female. She grabs Stevie and body slams him to the floor. She pulls him up with ease and stands him up on his feet.

"Why do you look like this?" a third monster says. He walks up and grabs Stevie by the face, turning his head back and forth to examine him.

"That energy drink did this to me," Stevie says. He is clearly talking through pain. The female monster has his arms pinned behind his back.

"The Black Skull of Death did this to us, though, right?" the monster says, taking a step back. "But why do you look different?"

"It doesn't matter, Jeff," the monster holding me says. "Let's just take them to Vince. I'm getting horny. I wanna see if he wants to wreck this bitch's pussy."

He licks the side of my face with his disgusting tongue. I see Stevie struggling to pull free, but that female has a good grip on him.

They drag us over to where Vince and the other monster are still going at it. They are panting and growling, smacking and biting each other. It's disgusting to watch. But finally Vince pulls his mutilated-looking cock out and let's his discolored man-juice fly. Most of it lands on the female monster, but some shoots wildly, going right past me. I think if any of it landed on me I would have thrown up.

"Yes!" he yells. "That's what I'm fucking talking about!"

He grabs an energy drink and chugs the whole can. Tossing it behind him, he turns his attention to us.

"Now, what do we have here?" he walks over to Stevie first. "Little Stevie. Is that you? I can see some things have been happening for you today too." He looks down and grabs Stevie's cock.

"Man, look at this dick! No wonder you're hanging out with him, Janet, as much as you love the cock. I bet you really love this big ass motherfucker!"

I can tell Stevie is looking at me, but I don't want to meet his gaze. I'm not sure what he thinks Vince might mean by that. Maybe he doesn't think anything of it and I'm being paranoid.

"Throw this little fucker on the floor. I have an idea," Vince tells the female monster.

She turns and slams him down on his face. Vince kicks him and forces him to roll over. When he does, Vince stands on Stevie's arms to immobilize him. He crouches down, right above his chest. His weird dong is all in Stevie's face, and no matter how he turns his head, he can't quite get away from it. Vince laughs as he smacks Stevie in the face with the head of his dick. His nasty sperm is still dripping out of the end.

"I could make you suck my dick right here," Vince says. He rubs the glistening head of his shlong on Stevie's lips, but Stevie keeps his mouth closed tight. "But, lucky for you I just had a nice piece of ass. So, because I'm feeling all nice and shit, I'm going to hook you up."

Vince stands up and puts his full weight on Stevie's arms. Stevie screams out in pain. Vince turns and grabs me from Craig. He throws me down onto Stevie.

"Give this man a blow job, bitch," Vince says. "I know he ain't ever had one before and I know that you're a fucking pro at gobbling some knob."

I look up at Stevie's face. He looks as scared as I feel.

"You don't have to do this," he says to me.

"Oh, yes you do, bitch," Vince says. He grabs me by the hair and pulls my head up.

"Let her go!" Stevie yells. He tries to get up, but the monsters are all over him, stomping him back down.

"If you don't start sucking this man's big fucking dick, me and my two friends are going to plug all of your holes with our big fucking dicks. And we will fuck you to death, do you hear me?" Vince is so close to my face that I can smell the energy drink's medicinal smell. I'm crying now, but I manage a feeble *yes.*

He drops me back down onto Stevie, but I don't look up at him this time. I just grab his big, flaccid cock and get to work. It doesn't stay limp for long. Let's be honest, Vince is right, I am really good at this. And under different circumstances, I would be really enjoying it. As it is, I do not hate it. Having an audience doesn't bother me either. I've done a lot worse in front of an audience before. But forcing Stevie into this is wrong. This is just another reason Vince is an asshole.

It doesn't take long before I feel Stevie's body start to tense up. I know he's getting ready to cum. I pull away and Vince shoves my head back down.

"Swallow that shit, bitch. Just like you did mine."

I do as he says. I bring Stevie to ejaculation and try to swallow it down. It's a lot, and tastes unusual. When he's done, I pull away and some of it runs out of my mouth.

"Oh my god that made me so fucking hard!" Vince says.

"Damn, bitch, you got some skills," Jeff says. "You should be in porn."

I look over and I see the three monster guys with erections in their hands, and I'm thinking Vince isn't going to let me go that easy.

"Now see, you got me all excited," Vince says. "Looks like I'm gonna have to fuck you after all."

Out of nowhere, I hear a gunshot and I'm sprayed with blood. Half of Craig's head is now missing. We all look in the direction the shot came from and it's the cashier. I forgot about that dude. I guess I assumed he was dead or something.

"What did you do?" Vince screams. He's looking at Craig's body as it falls to the floor.

"Come on," I say to Stevie. I pull on his hand. "While they're distracted, we should go."

The monsters start to move in on the cashier and Stevie sits up. I look over and the cashier is fumbling with the gun. Maybe he's trying to reload it, I don't know.

We head for the door and I hear Vince yelling to stop us. I don't even turn around to look, I just keep going. I don't quite make it to the door when I'm thrown to the ground. I roll over and see Stevie and a female monster, the one Vince was fucking, rolling around grappling. I don't know where Stevie pulls the strength from, but I watch as he picks the female up and choke slams her. He's got the advantage, and he uses it. He wails on her face. He pounds away, and it's brutal. But then I notice Vince has the cashier and he's pointing at us, and talking to Jeff.

"Stevie!" I yell. "We have to go!"

He looks up at me with a confused look on his face. Then he looks behind him, to where I am pointing, at Vince and his remaining friends. He nods and runs over to me. He grabs me up in his arms and cradles me like a baby, and we're out the door. I look back once we're on the street and it doesn't look like anyone is following us.

HAROLD

"Look man, this gun is one hundred and twenty five dollars," Jessie says to me. I don't know anything about guns so I don't know if I'm getting ripped off or not. "Look Harry, I got a few bullets I can throw in with it. That's it, cheapest I got, take it or leave it.'

"I wish people would call me Harold,' I say, which is pointless. I'll be hairy Harry Harrison forever, as long as I live in a piece of shit town like this and Vince and his friends are here.

"Whatever dude. Quit looking at the gun like you want to suck its dick," Jessie says. Fuck this dude. He doesn't even realize he's watching a vigilante being born in his midst.

"Yeah, give me the fucking thing," I say. I pull the wad of cash out of my pants pocket, one hundred and twenty five bucks, it's all I have. I had been saving for a while, mainly from cutting some of the neighbors grass. It's the freaking twenty first century, who pays five bucks to have their grass cut? I should stand up for myself and charge more. Anyway, I had my eye on an original Cobra Terror Dome on E-bay, but that shit Vince pulled today was the last straw. Doesn't he know comic shops only got in a select few copies of the gold foiled, 3-d embossed, variant sketch cover of Wolverine where he's from an alternate time-line and he's pregnant with Jean Grey's baby? Who would take a shit on a book like that? I can't send that off to the Comic's Grading Company like that. Vince has to be stopped.

"Here's a box with a few shells in it.' Jessie says. "You do know how to use that thing, right?"

"Uh yeah, I guess I do."

"Okay, cool. Later Harry, I've got a girl coming over so you need to split." He says, basically blowing me off. I don't care, I tuck the gun into the waist band of my jeans and leave Jessie's apartment. I feel like a bad ass, like Han Solo. I hope the safety is on so I don't blow my dick off.

A guy I know said his girlfriend Lisa's sister Gwen is supposed to be partying with Vince and his goon squad. Why anyone would chose to hang out with those assholes I don't know. But, I know why they would want to hang out with her, she's smoking hot, like Black Widow with blonde hair or Buffy the Vampire Slayer, the Kristy Swanson one. I remember last summer, when I was near the lake. I was pretending I was Luke Skywalker running through the forests on the moon of Endor. When I got near the water, I heard some people talking. I quietly snuck around to get a look, and it was that guy's girlfriend, Lisa, and her sister Gwen. They were skinny dipping; it was an instant erection for me. I started imagining Gwen was princess Leia and her sister Lisa was a sister nobody knew about, a triplet maybe. So, here I was, Luke Skywalker, stroking my dick to Princess Leia and her sister, naked. Then I realized that would make them my sisters too. That made me even harder. Everybody knew one of the hottest parts of Star Wars is when it's revealed that Luke and Leia were actually brother and sister and that they had been making out in Empire Strikes Back.

While I'm thinking about that time at the lake, I walk into Huck's. This older mom lady gives me a nasty look and I realize I've got a raging boner pushing against my pants. I try to hide it, but it's awkward. I make it past the lady and to the drink cooler. I bet once I get rid of that dickhead Vince, the chicks he's partying with will want to have sex with me. I touch the handle of the gun under my shirt and think maybe I won't give them a choice.

MOTHER FUCKING BLACK SKULL OF DEATH

I don't know how long I'm standing at the drink cooler for, lost in my thoughts and stroking the handle of the gun, before somebody snaps me out of it.

"Hey Harry, what the fuck are you doing man?" someone says behind me. I turn and see Josh, who's wearing his Hucks uniform so I guess he's working today. I pull my shirt down to make sure the gun is hidden.

"Nothing man, I was just day dreaming," I tell him.

"I thought you were jacking off for a minute there," Josh says.

"What? Naw, fuck you dude," I say. I open the freezer door and grab a Mother Fucking Black Skull of Death, the 32 oz. Big-Azz can.

I take it up and sit it on the counter. By this time Josh is behind the register.

"What are you doing tonight?" he asks me as he rings up my drink. I think about the gun and how I could just take this drink if I wanted to. But that is a villain thing to do, and I'm trying to be a hero.

"Nothing much really," I say back.

"Oh, you ever let another dude watch you jack off before?"

"What? No!" What's wrong with guy?

"I'll show you some naked pictures of my sister. Come on man, you know she's hot," he says. He's right, she is hot, but not that hot.

"No, thanks, man," I say and grab my drink. "You're a freak dude." I tell him as I back away from the counter. He laughs and I exit the store.

Having this gun has got me really thinking some terrible thoughts. It's almost as if it's the ring from Lord of the Rings. I don't want to turn into Smegal, I just need to get this job done and get rid of this thing.

I open up my Mother Fucking Black Skull of Death and take a great big chug. It tastes a little funny, I guess it's been in the cooler for awhile or something, maybe it got hot and then re-chilled. It's not too bad, though, and I start chugging it down.

Before I know it I find myself at the house. It's oddly quiet, not at all what I would have expected from a party. I can only assume what a party is like since I've never actually been to one. In the movies they're always really wild and crazy, with people inside and out being jack-asses.

As I'm walking up to the front door I am trying to think of how this will probably go. 'Hey, let me in. I need to talk to Vince,' probably won't really cut it. But the front door is actually open, so that part is easy enough.

A noise from the hallway startles me and I pull the gun out. I'm shaking, I'm so nervous. I feel like I need to poop. I chugged that whole can of Black Skull and so now I need to pee too.

Hesitantly, I walk to the hallway. The noise is coming from a room in the back of the house. I slowly creep towards the room. I don't understand why there isn't anyone else here if this is a party, but I keep moving, just hoping Vince is in that room.

The door to the room is broken off and lying on the floor, so once I'm close enough I see right inside. I don't know what the fuck that thing is in there, but it looks like a huge monster. Its body is a dingy gray, and rocky. It's naked, and thrusting it's hips like it's fucking someone. It's grunting, and maybe crying? I shift my weight to turn and leave and the floor creaks. The thing stops thrusting and turns and looks at me and I piss down the front of my pants. It opens the mouth on its disfigured face and lets out a roar. I don't see any teeth, which I find odd. I don't put much thought into it, I just turn to run. As I turn, I catch a glimpse of what the monster might have been fucking; it looked like a dead chick.

I don't have time to investigate. I run as fast as my scrawny legs let me. I hear the thing tearing out after me. When I get to the front door and outside, I still don't feel safe. I keep pumping my legs into the night.

VINCE

I drag the two monstrous corpses next to each other and think, *maybe I should be sad*, but all I can hear is Jeff and that other monster bitch fucking. It is very distracting.

I chug a fucking Black Skull and think about how not too long ago I was pounding away on this dead bitch's pussy. Something about this energy drink turning us into monsters makes me fucking horny as fuck. Well, I guess it does it to all of us. So, fucking this monster bitch was awesome, especially when she ripped that dude's head off and poured his blood on her.

Thinking about that shit makes me hard again. I reach down and touch the dead bitch's pussy. It's still kinda warm. I pick her body up and lay her over Craig's body, so her ass is in the air. At first, I figure her butthole is already pointing right at me; I'll just stick my cock in there. She's dead, so she won't try to stop me like most girls do. But she must have shit herself when she died, because that weird, green colored shit is all over her. And it stinks like something awful.

I kick her body off of Craig's corpse and the idea hits me to just stick my cock in him, just face fuck the shit out of him. But Jeff and that bitch are being so annoying, it's distracting. Fuck this. Why should I be over here fucking corpses when there are two live motherfuckers over there? I walk to the beer section where they are at. The monster bitch is on the floor, lying on her back, with Jeff tearing up her pussy.

"Gimmie a hole, bitch," I say to her. They don't stop fucking, but they both look at me. My dick is rock-hard and right above her head. She's looking right at it. "You're gonna take this motherfucker, but I'm gonna let you choose where."

"Come on man, let me finish first," Jeff says.

"I'm not telling you to stop, but if she doesn't give me a place to put this, you will," I say to him. He looks at me and I can tell he feels big and bad now that he's a fucking monster, but he's not that big and bad. It doesn't matter, because she reaches up and grabs my dick and takes it in her mouth.

I feel a lot better after I finish fucking this bitch's mouth. Now that we've all gotten that out of the way, I tell them it's time to go.

"I want some more fucking Black Skull of Death," I say to them. "And I want to find Stevie and that cunt. I'm going to destroy both of their assholes."

Jeff and the bitch are growling and getting riled up again. We set out into the night.

STEVIE

"What in the hell is happening around here?" Janet asks. I don't know if she is asking me or just thinking out loud. I don't look at her. I haven't really looked at her since we left the Marathon. I feel bad, and embarrassed, and ashamed. I don't know what to do with myself, or with her. I'm pretty uncomfortable, especially being in her bedroom. I should never have agreed to come here, but where else could I go? Maybe I should have went and hid in the woods.

"Just relax, Stevie. Everything will be okay," she says. She puts her hand on my knee. I flinch away.

"I'm sorry," I say. I feel like an idiot. I have a Hello Kitty beach towel wrapped around me and I am sitting on her bedroom floor. There's almost not enough room in here for me.

"You don't have anything to be sorry for," she says.

"Yes, I do. What happened at the store, that shit was just plain wrong."

"But it wasn't your fault," she says. She scoots around to sit in front of me. "That was Vince and his friends. They are terrible people."

"I know, I just feel awful about it," I say. I raise my head slightly and look at her, she's smiling.

"Don't feel awful, it was fine," she says. "I didn't mind doing it." She lowers her head shyly.

"Why don't you two just fuck already and get it over with?" something said from behind me. I turned around. I didn't think anyone else was in the room. I didn't see anybody.

"What was that?" I asked.

"I'm sorry, that was my friend Stacy. She's not very nice sometimes."

"But I don't see anybody," I say, turning back to look at her. Something taps me on the back of my head.

"I'm right here, big man," the small voice says again. I turn around and standing on the bed is a stuffed doll. It is looking right at me, hands on its hips and everything. I feel like I should be freaking out about this, but with everything that has happened tonight, this doesn't bother me at all.

"Man, you are one big boy," the doll says to me. "I bet you got a big cock don't you?"

"Stacy!" Janet says. "Don't talk to him like that."

I turn back around to face Janet.

"Why are you even friends with this thing?" I ask.

"Hey, fuck you buddy!" Stacy says.

"She's not always like this," Janet says. "And besides, we've been together a long time."

"Yeah, she may be sucking your dick or fucking you now, but we will still be friends even when she's giving it to the next guy," Stacy says. She really is a bitch.

"You don't have to be so mean," Janet says. "Where is Mr. Snugs?"

A lump moves underneath the blanket on the bed. I watch as it moves towards the pillows at the headboard. A brown stuffed bear pops its head out from under the blanket.

"I'm right here, Janet," the bear says.

"Come on out and say hi to Stevie," Janet says. I watch this little brown bear crawl out from under the covers and cautiously walk over to the edge of the bed. The poor thing looks afraid, but of what, I'm not sure. Reason would indicate me, I am big and intimidating, I suppose, but as the bear nears Stacy, she turns towards him and he flinches.

"Hey, how's it going?" I ask the little thing. Before it can answer, I'm struck with a terrible pain. My body is demanding an energy drink. My stomach is cramping. I turn towards Janet. "I have to go find some Black Skull of Death."

"Okay, let's go then," she says.

"You need to stay here. After what happened last time, I don't want to risk running into Vince with you around."

TERRENCE

"Dammit, dog! Where the hell you at," I yell. Where is that stupid mutt? I've got my cock all lathered with peanut butter, and this shit ain't gonna lick itself off.

I pound my fist on the table and finally that damn piece of shit dog is dragging its ass around the corner.

"Get your ass over here!" I yell at him again. I thrust my dick towards him. I don't know what his problem is. He knows what to do.

I pick up a Mother Fucking Black Skull of Death. God, I love these things. The stupid dog finally comes over and starts to lick my junk. I open the drink, but set it down. His sandpaper tongue feels great on my rock-hard cock. While the dog is licking on my shaft, I try to get my erection in its mouth. One of its teeth scrapes my dick and I jump up, smacking the stupid thing away.

"What the fuck!" I yell. I try to swing at the piece of shit and it jumps back just in time, but the little motherfucker runs into the leg of the table and knocks my drink over.

"Just fucking great!" I look down and see some blood on my dick. That's more important than any energy drink. "Can this night get any fucking worse?"

I walk over to the sink and wet a rag to clean my cock off. It turns out it was just a small scratch, no biggie. I turn around and that dumb fucking dog is licking up all of my spilled energy drink. Great, now I'm going to have to go to the fucking store again. I grab the roll of paper towels and walk over to the mess.

"Get the fuck out of here!" I say to the dumb mutt as I kick him in his asshole. He runs off.

Once I get the floor and table clean, it's time to punish that dog. One for making this mess, and two because I didn't get off yet.

"Where'd you get yourself to, you little motherfucker," I ask as I'm walking through the house. "Come on out. I'm gonna punish that asshole of yours."

I hear whimpering and growling coming from one of the back rooms. For some reason the door is pushed closed.

"You come on out and I'll be gentle with you," I say, as I push the door open. "If I have to hunt you down, then it's gonna be rough."

The room is dark and for whatever reason the light seems to be out. I can see that stupid shit in the corner. I unbuckle my belt and pull it free from my belt loops. I let my pants fall off and I step out of them. I pull my underwear off too. I'm getting hard just thinking about what's getting ready to happen. I snap the belt in excitement and I can see the shape of the dog move.

"Alright, you little bitch, come to daddy," I keep my voice gentle for now, cause it's about to get rough. The dog gets up, and he seems bigger. I think he's standing on his hind legs, because he looks taller than me! Something hits me and I'm knocked out of the room.

"What the fuck was that?" I say. I get up off the floor, rubbing my head. The thing is on me instantly. It kinda looks like my stupid dog, but it's huge! It's standing up on its back legs and its front paws are out like vicious claws. The thing is thick with muscles and it's got a giant dick hovering over my head.

"I'm sorry, oh god, I'm sorry for everything! Please, I was just having some fun! Please don't hurt me, please!" I beg. It just snarls at me. Drool pours out of its mouth.

It reaches down and grabs me by my dick and lifts me into the air. I kick my legs and flail my arms. I feel like my cock is gonna rip off! First, I'm slammed onto my back. Then it lifts me again and throws me into a wall. I almost lose consciousness. My vision is going dark. I'm up on my hands and knees when I feel a clawed paw wrap around my head and smash my face into the floor. I start screaming when I feel the monster's cock shoving into my asshole.

LYNN

I knew the old bats would have something to say when I sat a can of Mother Fucking Black Skull of Death on the table, especially Sharon. She is the most uptight, prissiest, bitch I've ever met, and at 79 years old, I've met a lot of people.

"Lynn, you shouldn't be drinking that stuff," Margaret says.

"It's fine," I say. I take a big chug. "I was smoking some weed on the way over and I had cottonmouth like a motherfucker."

"Lynn! Don't talk about doing marijuana," Margret said her voice a loud whisper.

"Oh, it's okay," I tell her. "What can they do, put me in jail? I'm too old to give a shit."

"Can you please watch your language?" Sharon says. She rolls her eyes at me, and then looks down at her bingo cards. Then I realize I'm so stoned, I forgot to stop and get some bingo cards on the way in. It's fine though. That whole 22 oz. can has gone right through me.

"I've gotta go piss," I say to no one in particular. I can feel Sharon rolling her eyes again.

As I walk through the crowd of old people, my stomach bubbles. I am glad I'm already on my way to the bathroom. I wouldn't want to have another accident, especially not here. Some of these old bitches would never let me live that down. I would have to hear about it every day until they finally die, or I do.

Just as I reach the hallway where the bathrooms are, I see George Staples. George is hot for an 80-year-old man, but he fucks like a dead fish. I hope he doesn't turn around and see me. He's preoccupied talking to Stella Fritz. That's a lost cause for him. Stella has a 40-year-old man on the side that only a few of us know about. Everybody knows how terrible George is in the sack. The only reason any of us ever fuck him is because he's easy, and he's married to

Sharon. I'll take a bad fuck from him almost any chance I can get just to be a bitch to her, but that's not on my mind right now. I manage to get past him and into the ladies room. My stomach is making some terrible noises and I think I'm just in time, except the one stall available is disgusting and there's somebody in the handicapped stall.

"Are you almost done in there?" I ask, as I tap on the door.

"Yes, dear, give me just a second more," an extremely frail voice said. There's no doubt that I'm an old lady, but I'm not like most of them around the bingo hall. These women act helpless, almost invalid. It's like they have one foot in the grave and the other foot they need somebody to take care of.

"Oh, dear," I hear her say, "Oh, my."

"Is there anything I can help you with?" I ask her. My patience is about at its end.

"Oh, no, dear," she says. She's laboring for breath like most normal people do after running a marathon. "I'm almost done. Oh, my!"

I hear a crash and a lot of commotion.

Without saying anything, I pull on the handle and the door pops open. Everything in this place needs to be repaired or replaced and the locks on the bathroom stalls are no exception.

Opening the door, I see an old lady sprawled out on the bathroom floor, her bloomers around her ankles, and her walker on its side nearby. She hasn't even flushed yet, and I have to say that it's some foul shit.

"I was trying to pull my undees up and I lost my balance," she says. I reach over and flush the toilet. That's when I almost shit myself.

"I'm sorry. I will help you up," I tell her. "But first, I have to take care of this."

I step over the helpless old lady and undo my pants.

"Oh, my. This is a bit uncomfortable," she says. She turns her eyes away.

"Come on, I don't have anything you haven't seen a million times," I say. Why are old people such prudes? I sit my boney ass down on the still warm toilet seat just in the nick of time.

A small explosion exits my rear and I'm actually a little embarrassed. "I'm so sorry about this."

My butt burns as more liquid than solid pours out.

"I understand, but oh my, what have you been eating?" she says, almost the exact moment the smell hits.

It feels really good to empty my bowels, but at the same time it feels awful. I'm beginning to think I might have to go to the doctor.

"Oh, my word!" the old lady says. She tries to get to her feet. She struggles a lot, but it's not getting her anywhere. "Oh, please, I can't breathe. I need to get out of here!"

"I know, I can't breathe either. Sorry," that's when the pain begins. I double over, wrapping my arms around my stomach. A giant fart escapes my rear, but I'm not even embarrassed. I couldn't care less right now. I let out a scream. My eyes are clinched tight and tears are running out at the edges. My muscles and bones are in agony. I scream some more and open my eyes a little. I can see a terrified look on the old woman's face. My legs crack and they are changing. My body seems to be growing! I jump up from the toilet and let out a monstrous growl. The old lady screams, but I don't care! I pick up her walker and start bashing her with it. I slam it down on her face over and over again. Every time I see a muscle on her body twitch, I slam it down again!

Once I feel satisfied, I launch the mangled walker at the stall door. I start to walk, but my panties and pants are wrapped around my ankles, so I stumble. I crash through the stall dividers and smash into the other toilet. The porcelain breaks under me and piss and shit spill out. I don't care though. I reach down and rip my pants off. I need something to drink. I need some Mother Fucking Black Skull of Death!

I smash through the bathroom door and the first person I see is George. He looks at me with a mixture of confusion and disbelief.

"Lynn? Is that you?" he asks me. I jump on him. My crotch hits him in the face and he falls on his back, my legs on either side of his head.

"You want to fuck again?" I ask him. I laugh and then grab his head and rip it off his shoulders. The bingo hall erupts into screaming madness.

I throw George's severed head at a stampede of canes and walkers. It starts a domino effect. Old people are tripping over each other. Some of the more spry ones are trampling the ones that have fallen. I jump into the middle of it. I land on a pile of screaming old people. Bones and colostomy bags are popping under my feet.

I let most of the old farts go. I figure if they make it out of here without having a heart attack or stroke, they'll probably only have a few more years anyway. I'm looking for one person in particular. I push and shove away the elderly as they shit themselves in their diapers. I grab an oxygen tank and rip it away from an old bastard. Then I see her — Sharon. I throw the oxygen tank at her feet and she falls to the ground, hard. I'm pretty sure I can hear her hip cracking.

I jump and land over top of her, my feet planted on either side of her body. She's screaming and crying, begging me not to kill her. I'm not going to kill her, I just want to have some fun. I grab her head and shove her face into my vagina.

"Come on, bitch, let's see if you can do this better than your husband," I say.

I start rubbing her face in my pussy. It feels good. Her arms are flailing, hitting me, and trying to get me to stop. I don't. I use her face to masturbate, and I'm not gentle. I really get her in there, and it feels awesome. I growl and moan, and when I'm done, I pull her face away. Her nose is twisted and broken. Blood is coming out of the nostrils. Both her lips are busted and bleeding and she's passed out. Maybe it was from lack of oxygen, or maybe it was just from the humiliation. Either way, she definitely did a better job than her husband.

I drop her body to the floor and take off into the night, in search of some Black Skull of Death.

JANET

I hang back as much as I can and watch Stevie from a distance. He told me to stay at my house, and I know he just wants to protect me, but I'm worried about him too.

"This is ridiculously stupid," Stacy says from behind me. I brought her and Mr. Snugs with me in a backpack. I don't know if it was a good idea though, especially since Stacy won't stay quiet.

"Please, keep your voice down," I say to her again. "And this isn't stupid, he might need our help."

"Really? The guy is freakin' huge. He's like a big, buff monster. What could we possibly help him with?" Stacy says.

"I know he's a big scary guy," I tell her. "But you haven't seen those other people. They are really crazy-looking."

"That is not helping your case at all," she says. I hear her mumble something else, but I quit listening. I lost track of Stevie. We're right around the corner from Speedway, but I never saw him go that direction. I should have left these distractions at home.

"What are you doing here?" I hear Stevie say from behind me. I turn around and face him. "I told you to stay back at your place."

"I know, I know, but I'm worried about you," I tell him. "I want to be here in case you need help. There's three of them and only one of you."

He shakes his head. I don't know if he's mad or what, and before I can find out, something hits me and throws me across the sidewalk.

"Janet!" Stevie screams. I roll over and see one of the big, monster-looking guys, or actually, it's a chick.

"Who the fuck are you?" she says. Stevie doesn't even give her an answer, he just attacks. As I watch him punch her in the face savagely, I realize she isn't one of the monsters that were with Vince earlier.

"Holy shit," Stacy says. "What the crap is that thing?"

"She's like one of the monsters we dealt with earlier, but I don't recognize her," I tell Stacy.

"She would have killed us if it weren't for Stevie," Mr. Snugs says, finally making an appearance.

"Yeah, but if we wouldn't have been out here, it wouldn't have been a problem," Stacy says.

I decide to ignore them both. I watch as Stevie and this other monster battle it out. They toss each other around, slamming one another onto the pavement and parked cars. Stevie seems to be holding his own, but he's not exactly winning. Then an idea occurs to me, *what if he was to have some Black Skull of Death?*

I take off towards Speedway. I hear the two of them continuing to fight behind me and wonder why nobody has come out to see what all the noise is. It seems as though someone would have called the police by now.

Speedway is lit up like any other day, but the place looks dead. There are not too many people out at this time of night. Inside, there's a young dude behind the counter who barely acknowledges my existence. I try to act casual and walk over to the drink coolers. It's looking like they're running pretty low on the Black Skull, but there are a few, so that's all that matters. I set four of them on the counter.

"Guess you plan on being up for awhile, huh?" the young dude says.

"Well, they're not all for me."

"It's whatever. I'm not judging," he says, ringing them up and putting them in a plastic bag. "These things sure are popular though. You got a Speedy card?"

"No, I forgot it at home," I say, hoping this dude would speed it up a little.

After the transaction, he holds the bag out for me. I grab it, but he doesn't let go.

"Since you're going to be up late tonight anyway, you wanna party?" the guy says with a goofy grin.

I open my mouth to answer him, but something hits the side of the store, causing the entire place to shake.

"What the fuck was that?" he says, letting go of my drinks. I don't answer. I just take my bag and run for the door.

I'm not outside two seconds before the monster Stevie is fighting comes flying into the parking lot, slamming into one of the columns supporting the roof over the gas pumps. Stevie comes walking from around the corner.

"Hey, I got you something," I say, but he ignores me. I watch as he grabs a hold of the Red box machine and yanks it out of the ground. He hoists it up into the air and turns towards the monster. From out of nowhere, another monster slams into Stevie, knocking him into one of Speedway's walls and causing him to drop the Red box machine. It's Jeff. I turn and see Vince and his other monster pals walking up.

"Well, well, well," he says in an evil voice. "This is a nice surprise."

I turn and run back into the store. I walk behind the counter and there is the cashier, sitting on the floor with a revolver in his hands.

"What are those things out there?" he asked me.

"I don't know, monsters of some kind," I set my backpack down and get a Black Skull of Death out of the plastic bag. "And I'm getting ready to become one."

VINCE

I must be one lucky motherfucker. I'm just going out to get some Mother Fucking Black Skull of Death and I walk right into the motherfucker I want to kill most, and his girlfriend. But I won't be killing her, at least not at first. But, wait a second, who is this monster?

"Hey, Jeff," I call out. He turns and looks at me. "We've got another fucked up monster!"

I walk over to the thing lying by the gas pumps and kick it so it rolls over.

"Hey, dude! It's another bitch!" I yell to Jeff. "She is fucked up looking."

Jeff walks up and gets a good look at this monster.

"Oh yeah, she is definitely fugly," Jeff says.

"Yeah, I don't care about fucking her, so you know something is wrong with her!" We both laugh, because I'm a funny motherfucker.

"Check this out," I say. I grab the nearest nozzle and hit the button for the expensive shit. I'm not paying for it, so it doesn't matter. She starts twitching when the gasoline hits her.

"Gimmie a light," I say to Jeff. I hold my free hand out to him.

"I don't smoke, dude," he says to me. I shoot him an impatient look.

"Then take your ass inside and get me a lighter. You're killing the fun," I just don't know about some people.

I watched this fucked up bitch as I drown her in gas. She's squealing and trying to cover her sensitive parts. I hear a bunch of commotion behind me and turn to see little fuckin' Stevie still wants to play.

I hang back and watch as he and Jeff slaps each other around like a couple of little girls. Speaking of which, where is that bitch that was hanging out with us? It doesn't matter. Jeff seems to be delivering a pretty decent beat down to little Stevie. He'll have him sucking his cock in no time. I guess I'll have to go inside and get my own lighter. Might even have to find Janet, if she's hiding inside, I've got a little something for her ass.

"Oh, shit!" I yell as I duck to avoid whatever just came through the freakin' window. It's that bitch that was with us. She must have been inside the store. But who the fuck just launched her through the window?

I go to investigate, because I'm not scared of anybody. I don't care that they just threw the bitch out like she was nothing; I'll still kick their ass!

Somebody's climbing out the window, and looks like they're coming to me. Wait, is that Janet? She's huge, muscular and red-looking. She looks like a female version of Stevie. How did this happen? Why don't they look like me, or Jeff and Craig?

"Stevie!" she yells when she sees him lying under Jeff. He almost looks dead.

"I wouldn't worry about him, babe," I say to her. I jump between her and Jeff and Stevie. "But I got something here that I think you need."

She doesn't waste any time, she comes running right at me. I don't know if she's cocky or she thinks I won't hit a girl, but I lay her the fuck out quick. She falls back and slams onto the ground.

"Alright, bitch," I say to her. I grab her by her hair. She's practically unconscious from one punch! "Let's go get something to drink. Then we can get down to business."

"No, Janet!" I hear Stevie say. I don't even turn around; I just drag her into the store.

The store is a wreck, I guess from Janet and that bitch. I can see the drink cooler as soon as I walk into the store. It looks intact, so that's all that matters to me.

I drop Janet on the floor in front of the cooler and turn towards the glass door. I see the reflection of something big coming up behind me. My first thought is Stevie actually got away from Jeff, but that can't be him. This thing is too big.

I turn around and I am face to face with a giant teddy bear. Fuck this thing. I'm not fucking scared of it.

GINA

Tom is pawing on me like a child, grabbing on my boobs and trying to shove his tongue down my throat. I don't know why I agreed to come up to suck face hill with him, he's acting like a virgin. Tracy told me he had a long cock, she didn't tell me he didn't know what to do with it. Don't you hate that lame shit?

I push him off of me and he looks like a whipped puppy, I seriously think he's going to cry. I pick up my can of Mother fucking Black Skull of Death and chug the remainder.

"Ugh, how can you drink that nasty shit?" Tom asks me. I roll my eyes; this guy is turning into a real pussy.

I lean forward and put my hand on the back of his head. He smiles at me with a stupid, goofy grin. I pull his head down into my crotch.

He freaks out and pushes my hand away and lifts his head back up.

"What the hell?" he says. He looks disgusted."I don't do that sort of thing!"

"You don't eat pussy?" I say. Is this guy fucking kidding me? "Are you gay? You can tell me if you are its okay."

I don't really care to listen to what he has to say. I light up a cigarette and get out of the car. All I have on is my bra and underwear, and the night air feels good. I've gotten really hot out of nowhere, and it definitely wasn't from this whiner.

"Come on; just get back in the car. I'll show you I'm not gay, alright?" Tom says from behind me. I turn around and he has stripped off his pants and underwear. He really is packing; his dick does have some size to it. That makes things a little better.

I throw my cigarette down and walk back to the car. I take my bra off as I walk and Toms looking at my tits like it's the first times he's ever seen a pair. His dick is getting hard and I pull my panties off. They might be a little wet.

I gently ease him down onto the seat and tell him to scoot in. I climb on top of him and slide his dick in with ease. I go to town riding that big mother fucker like it's never been ridden before, then my stomach cramps. I stop and bend forward. His dick isn't so big that it hurts, but what was that? I feel like I need to fart, but I hold it in.

"You okay?" he says. "Did you, uh, you know?"

"Shut up," I tell him and start riding some more. I put my hands up on the roof of the car. My stomach rumbles like I've got bubble guts. I've got sensations going through my body I've never felt before. Some of it's painful, in my joints, and my head is on fire. I keep riding, but my body feels weird. My knuckles are cracking, my back is spasming.

"Are you cumming?" Tom says. I open my eyes and he looks like he's in pain.

I open my mouth to say something and instead I scream. I push out on the roof of the car and feel something give way. My head feels likes its splitting and my eyes are bulging out of my face.

I look up to see the sky where the roof of the car should be, and I see my hands. They're enormous and ugly. I stop moving and look at my arms, they're also huge and weird, covered in warts with lumps jutting out randomly. I look down at the rest of my body, at least my tits have grown too. My skin has changed to a dingy gray color.

Tom's eyes are wide and he's hyperventilating. I start riding him again.

"Are you cumming yet?" I ask. I laugh, and my voice is harsh, like I was gargling razors or smoked three packs a day.

As I ride Tom I can hear his bones crunching and grinding together. I think he might be dead and for some reason that doesn't bother me. Finally, I start cumming and it feels great. I let out a huge roar, I feel so primal, so monstrous.

I get up off of Tom and he's definitely dead. His body is smashed; his big dick is barely hanging on by a piece of skin. I just about ripped that sucker off.

"Holy fuck," someone says behind me. I turn to see a young guy, he looks familiar, and like maybe we went to school together. He's holding a gun and he's out of breath like he's been running. "There's another one of you monsters?" he says. I assume he's obviously talking about me, but what does he mean another one?

I step towards him and he weakly raises his gun. Something large charges up behind the guy and he fires the gun, not aiming or anything. He basically just shoots the ground.

The large thing behind the little guy is a freaking monster, and he looks a lot like me. He tackles the little guy and I almost feel sorry for him when I hear bones snapping, almost. This transformation has given me a blood lust.

The other monster stands up over the crumpled kid's body and I notice this big feller's monster erection. I wonder if I have a blood lust or perhaps it is just lust.

I run over to the monster just as he picks the guys body up off the ground. I slam into the big guy and grab his face, squishing the little guy in-between our bodies. The sides of his body split open at impact and blood splats out from in-between us two monsters. I smash the other monsters face with mine and shove my tongue down his throat, he reciprocates. He seems to be missing a lot of teeth, making his gums weirdly crater like.

I pull his head down my body, the little guys now dead body slides down too. The monster grabs me up by my waist and we move until my back slams against the car. I keep forcing his head down and I lift up my lower body. I use the car for support against my back and he grabs under my thighs and shoves his face into my pussy. He gums the shit out of me and I love it.

He shoves his face into me hard, and it feels like the car slides some. It doesn't matter, not right now. All that matters is this monster keeps doing what he's doing. Until I realize the car gives way from behind me. Since I was being supported by the car, I go with it. My monster man is still holding my legs up and shoving his face in my crotch. The two of us and the car tumble over the side of Suck Face Hill, which is more of a mountain than hill. I lash out, hoping to catch a hold of something. The ground races to meet us too quickly and I land with a sickening splat. I can't feel anything; I can't move anything except my eyes. I can see the monster guy where he landed not too far from me and he is twisted in a pretzel like way no human body should ever be. He's not moving either.

There's darkness creeping up on my vision. I should be worried that I'm about to die, but instead, all I can think about is a big ass can of Mother Fucking Black Skull of Death. Damn.

STEVIE

I can hardly breathe. I think my nose is broken, but I've never had a broken nose, so I can't say for sure. My body hurts. I wonder if some of this pain could be from broken ribs. I was doing okay against that one monster lady, I don't know who she was, but when she hit Janet, it just set me off. Jeff is just too much. Even watching Vince drag Janet away, I can't get myself riled up enough to knock Jeff off of me.

Oh, Janet, what have you done to yourself? Did you drink the Black Skull of Death? If so, why doesn't she look like Vince and those other guys? Instead, she looks like me.

I try one last time to give it my all, to remove Jeff from a position of power over me. Without warning, Jeff is gone and I get a little relief. I try to breathe deep and quickly realize the mistake in that, the pain in my sides make me think some of my ribs are broken.

Rolling over to my right, I see the female monster I was fighting earlier holding Jeff in a bear hug from behind. Jeff is thrashing and trying to break free, but she is displaying an insane amount of strength. She walks backwards as she carries him away from me.

Glass shatters from behind me. I wouldn't have thought there was any glass left in the store windows. I fight to get to my feet. It's a struggle. I don't think there is a single part of my body not screaming in agony.

I'm surprised when I look and see the reason the glass shattered, because Vince was thrown through it. I'm even more surprised when I see a giant teddy bear come climbing out the window. It is none other than Mr. Snugs, only he hasn't been changed by the Black Skull of Death like any of us were, instead it's just a really big Mr. Snugs.

"Help me," a strained voice says from behind me. I turn around. "Help me."

It's the female monster that's holding Jeff. She kicks something towards me. I reach down and pick up a small box of matches. I look up at her and she slowly nods her head. I pull a match out of the box.

"Don't you fucking do it," Vince says from behind me. "I'm going to kill every one of you pieces of shit."

Mr. Snugs grabs Vince by the throat and lifts him into the air. The giant teddy bear growls in his face. I see Janet climb out of the broken window, and I wonder why she didn't just use the door. I turn back to the woman who has Jeff. She mouths the words 'do it.'

I strike the match and toss it towards the two. They catch fire as the flame hits the fumes. It's so bright, I turn my head just in time to witness Vince try to punch Mr. Snugs and the giant teddy bear isn't even fazed. He just rips Vince in two like it's nothing.

I turn back and see Jeff rolling on the ground, screaming, and flailing his arms and legs. It's disgusting and I don't want to watch. I look around for the female monster. She is sitting on the ground, not making any noise as she burns alive. I guess I'll never know where she came from or why she sacrificed herself.

It doesn't take very long for Jeff to stop moving. Janet comes up to me and hugs me, it feels good.

"Why did you drink it?" I ask her.

"I wanted to help you. I didn't know what else to do," she says.

"I don't understand why you didn't turn out like Vince and the others," I say, but then it hits me. "Before they forced me to drink the Black Skull of Death, I was working on a chemistry experiment. My compound exploded. It must have absorbed into my skin and caused a different reaction with whatever chemical is in the drink."

"But how does that explain me?" Janet asks.

"Well, my guess is when Vince and them made you…uh,"

"Suck your cock?"

"Ah, yeah, that. By ingesting my semen, you put the counteracting chemical inside you."

"Oh, okay. That makes sense," she says. "But how do we explain Mr. Snugs?"

"I can explain that," the giant teddy bear says. "I've always been able to grow big like this; I just don't because it makes me mean. When I saw that man hurting you, I just couldn't help it. I had to do something."

Janet gave the big bear a hug. As she did, Mr. Snugs began to shrink down to normal size.

"Do you hear that?" I ask. There were sirens in the distance, and they were getting closer. "We need to go before they get here."

"Okay, let me run in here and grab Stacy," she said.

I watched her walk away, carrying the little teddy bear. I didn't know where we were going to go, but I was excited to be going with her.

HERMAN

"Come on, fellas, it's gotta be this way," Gomer said to us. That crazy old bastard, I don't know why ol' Jerry and I bother listening to anything he has to say. He's been talking all this nonsense about seeing Bigfoot out in some woods, behind his property in Shelby County. Pu-lease. But here we are, following him out here like a bunch of idiots.

"Hey, Herman, you don't reckon this ol' bastard is trying to get us out here so's he can kill us, do you?" Jerry says to me.

"I can hear you talking back there, shit bag," Gomer says. I hear something moving to our right. They hear it too, because they stop and turn their heads. Gomer raises the rifle in his hands, ready to take down whatever beast is in the woods with us. The noise is getting closer to us. Nobody makes a sound. Then everything is quiet. Nothing is moving in the woods.

"*Ah choo!*" Jerry sneezes, and then a freakin' monster jumps out of the woods in front of us. I don't think its Bigfoot, it almost resembles a dog, but it's walking upright and its freakin' crazy-looking! The thing lets out a crazy growl, louder than anything I've heard before. I can't help but notice the things got a pecker the size of a little kid's arm, and it's as hard as a tree stump.

Gomer points his rifle at the thing, but it smacks the gun away at the same time he pulls the trigger. The shot went wild, nowhere near hitting the thing. The monster towered over Gomer with its massive pecker staring him right in the face, and Jerry and I took off running.

Behind me I can hear Gomer as he screams in bright wet pain and begs us to help him.

I'm way too afraid to turn around and look, let alone turn my ass around to help, but I can hear him as the poor fuck's being choked out by what I can only assume is a ginormous dog-cock. Accompanying this are the sounds and reverberations like flesh being savagely ripped and rent. I don't need to look back to know it's bad.

I'm beating feet and I don't look back. You can if you want. Me? I don't need to. Don't want to.

Fuck that shit. All the way to next week and back you can.

... End

MOTHER FUCKING BLACK SKULL OF DEATH

MATTHEW VAUGHN is the author of *The ADHD Vampire* from Bizarro Pulp Press. He lives in Shelbyville, Kentucky and is the father of four little children, yet he and his wife are just big kids too. By day he maintains machines and robots, but, by night he is a writer of Bizarro fiction. You can keep up with his work:
http://mcvaughn.wordpress.com/
https://www.facebook.com/matthew.vaughn.12532

Also available from ~MorbidbookS~

In Print & Kindle Editions. Available at Amazon.com,

CreateSpace.com

and Barnes&Noble online:

~click on Kindle image for HYPERLINK~

~Maybe it had started when he was at university. He had a girlfriend in his final year that had gotten him into some weird stuff sexually then she left him for a guy with a bigger cock. The other guy was some gay looking chump with muscles and a tattoo; the pair had died in a car accident and Brian took a dump on their graves after each of their funerals. Fuck the both of them. But after she had left him he needed to fill the void of the newfound enjoyment of sickening sexual practices. Brain had purchased one of those 'real life' sex dolls online. Boy did the thing look real; you could bend it into any position and it came armed with enormous tits, willing mouth and a supposedly real feel pussy and anus. The packaging said to 'just add lubricant' but there was a problem. There was something missing; the smells, the tastes and the feel of real skin. You can't emulate that. So Brian set out to attempt to build a real life sex toy made from real life people.

~Keegan is a late-night public access radio show host, sexual deviant, and militant vegan. He has grown tired of his vegan cause being treated with apathy by the portly, meat-gorging, residents of the small town of Breen Gay, Wisconsin.

The time is ripe for Vegan vengeance. Keegan harvests roundworms from a local vagrant and mutates them using chemicals stolen from the meat packing plant. He infests the populace with the voracious, parasitic carnivores. Keegan knows that the only way for the people of Breen Gay to eliminate the parasites is to starve them of meat. It is with great expectation that he awaits the oncoming utopia of Veganism. However, the mutant roundworms will not die easily. The problems for the people of Breen Gay have only just begun.

~FOR SO LONG as anyone could remember, The Flagrant Five have ruled the land with an aggressive hand—enslaving children, destroying the wilderness—but Father Necrocious is tired of it all. One of his worst enemies (and a member of the Flagrant Five), Manservant Genesis, has escaped his imprisonment as a shadow.Therefore, he's enlisted the help of a ragtag group of fabricated Mercenaries to turn the fascists to shadows. The annual Dictators' Ball is pending (a battle in which children are used as pawns to determine the fate of the free world), and the brothers plan to stop the gala before it can commence. As they weave their way through the cartoonish landscape they will fight with their options to either trap the Flagrant Five with their shadow guns, or disobey their creator's orders and finally kill the Five for good.

~**The hands of the girls were inside of each-others zip front grey boiler suits** and they sat in the blood from where Sonny's face collided with the surface. The brunette had a finger smear of it next to her mouth.

"You two sluts put each other down and go tell Moira that Sonny's done. I'm coming in, just got a little business to attend to first."

As the two started to leave the big blond grabbed the shoulder of the red head and pulled her back.

"Not you Fire-Crotch, all this fucking blood has got me going." She started to unbuckle the belt on her camouflage hot pants. "Down you go, bitch!"

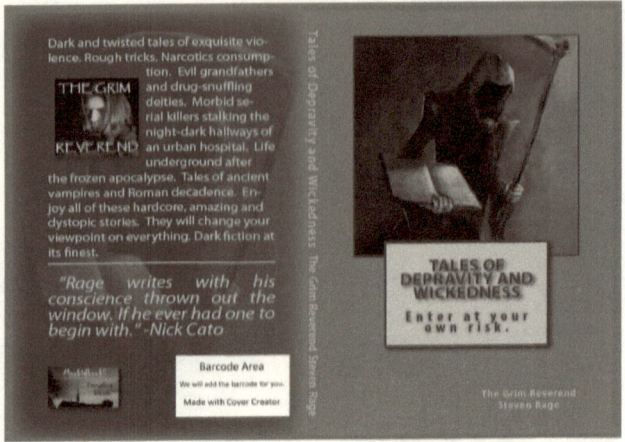

~Short stories from the Most Depraved Writer in Print. Dark and twisted tales of exquisite violence, rough tricks, narcotics consumption, evil ghosts and drug-snuffling demons. Evil grandfathers and animal-human hybrid clones. Morbid serial killer stalking night darkened hallways of an unsuspecting hospital. Life underground following the frozen apocalypse. Tales of ancient blood-thirsty vampires and Roman decadence. Enjoy all of the hardcore, dystopic, viscerally violent stories. Not for easily offended mamby-pambies. Dark fiction at its finest.

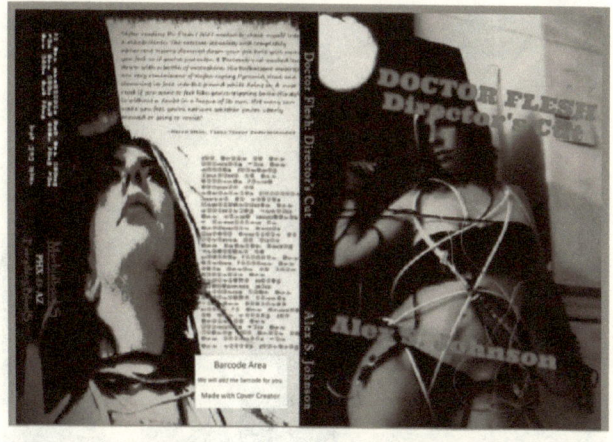

~From Alex S. Johnson, the author of **Bad Sunset, Wicked Candy and The Death Jazz,** comes a new vision in Bizarro horror. Imagine a TROMA film on meth and acid, one part cyberpunk, one part Franz Kafka, and three parts frankly unsuitable for a sane audience. "Will make you feel as if you've just eaten 8 Percocets and washed 'em down with a bottle of moonshine," says Necro Stein of Texas Terror Entertainment.

~**When the winds blew i felt them blowing through me,** when the land shook, it was my corpus that trembled. When the tides ebbed and flowed I became more shore and more sea. I was day and night as the sun and moon described the steps of their dancing within me. Just as I could see all the world at once, I was all of these things at once, and the motion of an entire world formed the foundation of my stillness. I'd travelled through the Sphere of Glammeth, descended through the Guardian, and then through the Grey-Man, fallen through a hole that pierced all the worlds.

~He had to have her the moment he saw her trachea ring. Six months later she was his lovely wife. He performed his duties as a husband and she as a wife. He tolerated a house filled with references to her late first husband and the children they had together. He put up with her prudish ways. He waited. He was patient. He planned. He was adaptable. He was rewarded over the course of a week in her basement. He turned his perverse sexual fantasies of worms and maggots and her lovely crusty trachea ring into a gruesome reality.

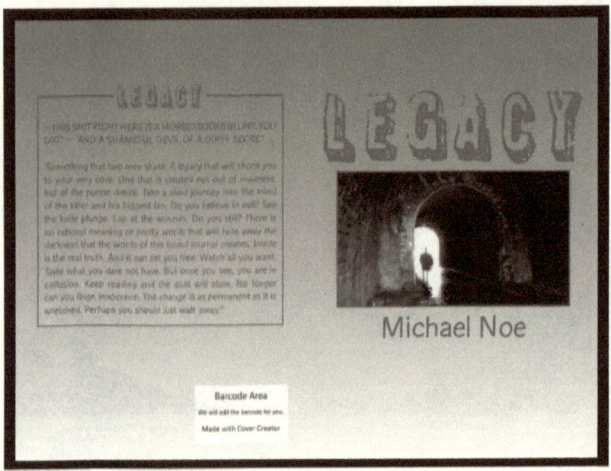

~A dirty shameful devil of a secret...

Something that two men share. A legacy that will shock you to your very core. One that is created not out of madness, but of the purest desire. Take a vivid journey into the mind of the killer and his biggest fan. Do you believe in evil? See the knife plunge. Lap at the wounds. Do you still? There is no rational meaning or pretty words that will hide away the darkness that the words of this found journal creates. Inside is the real truth. And it can set you free. Watch all you want. Taste what you dare not have.

~"The routine has this inherent tendency to perpetuate lies, and I speak only in thinly veiled euphemisms — hanging out with friends means going to the bar; being tired means too many sleepless nights on amphetamine; going grocery shopping means robbing Price Chopper blind; filling a prescription means visiting my dealer; going to the bank means pawning my possessions — but refer to them not as "lies;" rather, label them as weak excuses utilized to justify my erratic behaviours.

~I'm feeling down and dirty, feeling kind of mean, so I give those fans my middle finger. Those poor bastards go nuts. My team looks at me in awe. My coach frowns and the opposing one begins to furiously scratch out new plays. I see our opponents and I almost feel sorry for the poor bastards. Their fans can't help them. Their coach can't help them. I'm going to run them off their own track in front of their own fans and there is not one thing they can do about it.

~**Humanity is the devil is a deconstructed nightmare mixing David Lynch and snuff movies.** The plot revolves around a central character, Seth, who is set about a crusade against humanity which, for him, represents pure evil. Through random killings he and his cronies try to accelerate the end of the world, in order to provoke and defeat the Demiurge, the false God that is ruling the earth. As in Burroughs, logical language is replaced here with cut-scenes – sometimes to be taken literally – that plunge the reader into an extreme experience.

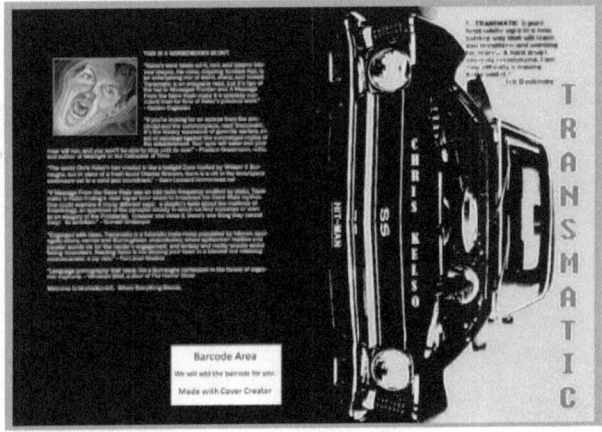

~"As a part-time hitman/ exterminator, Ignius Ellis's dream is to buy a candy-apple red Nova Supreme. In the process of trying to earn enough cash to make his dream come true he gets sucked into the rough world of Visitacion Valley, SF. When the tenants in his apartment complex reveal their various extracurricular activities this take an even more bizarre twist and Ellis soon becomes acquainted with the nightmarish Slave State dimension..."

~That's the last time she gets the bigger worm...

Once their flesh flakes away the angels collapse into puddles of hissing goop and withered petals blow into them hurried along by unseen winds. My spit looses its sweet taste to the black flavor of ash. The glowing birds in the bright orange sky burst into small sparkly novas. The sky itself weeps and tears, streaking down like a ruined painting as the dismal grey of life wheezes back before my eyes. I don't blink; praying silently for one last desperate sensation of the high. Lila feels it too. She writhes on the mattress next to me…

~**Within these twisted and perverted pages**, Johnson manages to demolish clichés with a jaded finesse that I've personally never encountered in written form. Another apparent talent is his effortless deconstruction of pop-culture allegories and references as found in his story "Vampussy." No one is safe or spared from his dagger sharp sarcasm and wit.

While not without its flaws, my appreciation for this kind of talent and voice is what made his writing so fun to read, even if he might possibly be out of his ever-loving mind.

MOTHER FUCKING BLACK SKULL OF DEATH

~In Garrett Cook's Murderland serial killers are idolized by society. Their deeds are followed obsessively by television pundits and the adoring public. A subculture has grown up around this phenomena, called "Reap." Laws are created to allow this activity to flourish, including designated "safe zones' where killers can practice their trade without fear of persecution. Fans of the top rated serial killers celebrate each new kill on social media and television. Programs glorify their deeds. The culture of Murderland is violent and mirrors our own violent society and its decadent obsessions.

~Born whole from the rectum of a dying patient, Morbid silently stalks the hospital's hallways, heinously dispatching the most helpless of patients and in the most painfully repulsive of manners. In the meantime, in order to pay for his family and home that includes his ghost step-father Sammy and his pet aborted fetus Chip, Westphal has to ingest mounds of dangerous narcotics to get through his night shifts. Barely hanging on to his Care Tech gig by his fingernails, the last thing Westphal needs is to be accused of Morbid's evil deeds. You, on the other hand, simply seek some solace from all Your diseases.

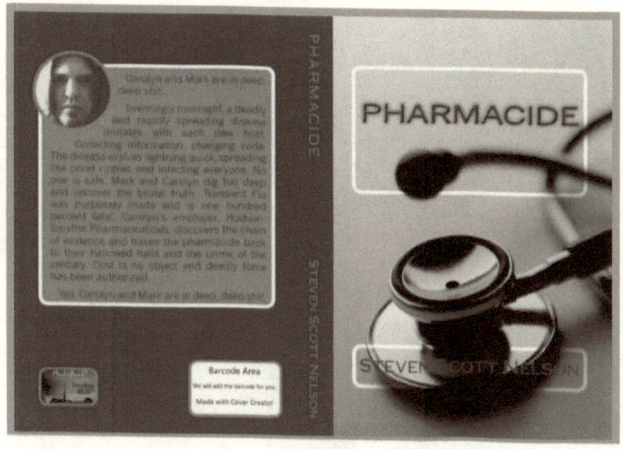

~It looks like Carolyn and Mark are in deep, deep shit...
Mark and Carolyn live in an alternate 1989 where Ronald
Reagan is on his fourth presidential term. The USA has a
rigid, long-standing caste system and abortions were never
made legal. Being homeless is a crime that is punishable by
imprisonment in Tent City. Most of Mark's ER patients are
inmates at this camp and are victims of a new disease
dubbed, Transient Flu. This deadly and rapidly spreading
disease mutates with each new host, collecting
information, changing code. The disease evolves lightning
quick, spreading like pond ripples...

~IMMANUEL THE CHRIST has some nerve. Jonah has already lost everyone he loves to Pilate the vampire and his Harbor drug violence. Jonah now trudges through his days staying as high on Plata as possible. He just wants to be left alone while he waits for his turn to die. The Christ has other plans for him. She sends Pedro, to assign Jonah to order the Herod to dismantle the Harbor's Plata trade. Jonah decides to run. But you can't run from God. As Jonah learns the hard way when the 'Edmund Fitzgerald' goes down in rough seas, with the reluctant prophet on board…

~Five Very Wicked Shorts. Brought to you with love and blood from The Grim Reverend Steven Rage, the 'Most Depraved Writer in Print'. ~

Through the sheer shock of his presentation, Rage forces readers to consider the alternatives, to look at the garbage in the streets, to see what is swept into the gutters at night right before all decent people awake to see another cleaned up version of the day. Depravity at its finest, but really the stories are loads of fun.

~**Pontius Pilate is cursed to be a vampire.** Life after life after life.~ And for the Plata dealing Pilate, his life is more like a death sentence. His only chance surviving is to keep on selling his monthly quota of Plata. This new man-made narcotic is a potent speed-ball designed to amp up the user, while also numbing the conscience into euphoric oblivion. To nullify the pain. To stifle the torture. To run and to hid from all the anguish inside. PILATE is a drug lord vampire in this re-telling of Christ's final days.

~Following religious folklore, parables, and beliefs, Rage presents the readers with a God who truly is the Shepherd that leaves no sheep behind. While this tale is deeply woven with the intricacies of a dark, drug-infested world ruled by evil forces, this is the story of a lost sheep. All are God's children, even most foulest of evil creatures who by their own will have become so through their spiritual and physical copulation with the Devil, and as such, in God's mercy, still are given a chance to be saved.

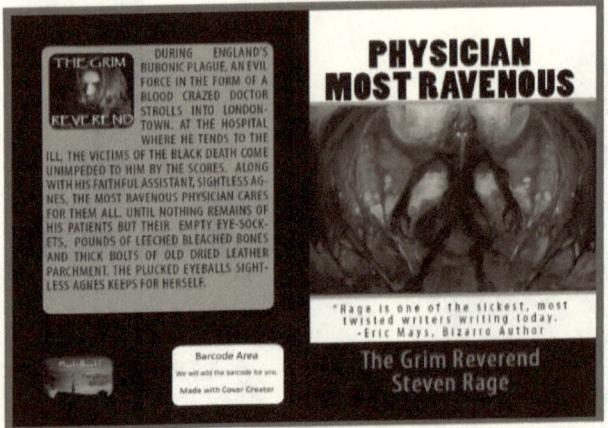

~During the height of England's Bubonic Plague an ancient Evil Force strolls into London-Town in the form of a would-be doctor. It could smell the blood from miles away, wanting only to help. At the hospital where he cares for the victims of this Black Death, the ill come to him unimpeded. They arrived and fell by the scores. With the help of his ever-faithful assistant, Sightless Agnes, a most ravenous cares for them all. Eating his way through an entire hospital, he treats them until there is nothing left. Nothing save their empty eye sockets, a few pounds of leeched bleached bones and some bolts of old dried-out flesh-leather parchment.

~New from MorbidbookS: **Where Everything Bleeds** is an instant collector's specimen and a certain stunner. ~ Be the first freak on your block to acquire this singular and unexpurgated exquisite culling of The Grim Reverend Steven Rage's favourite 'meds'. Enjoy this one-of-a-kind vivid look into the twisted mind of The Most Depraved Writer In Print as he captains you through the intoxicating stain of his wicked imagination. Included are numerous Photos, Paintings and Illustrations embellished with dramatic grayscale that enhance these iniquitous and magnificent   Dark   Fantasy   fables.

MATTHEW VAUGHN

www.ingramcontent.com/pod-product-compliance
Lightning Source LLC
Chambersburg PA
CBHW020738130626
46554CB00006B/2033